The Gotcha Smile

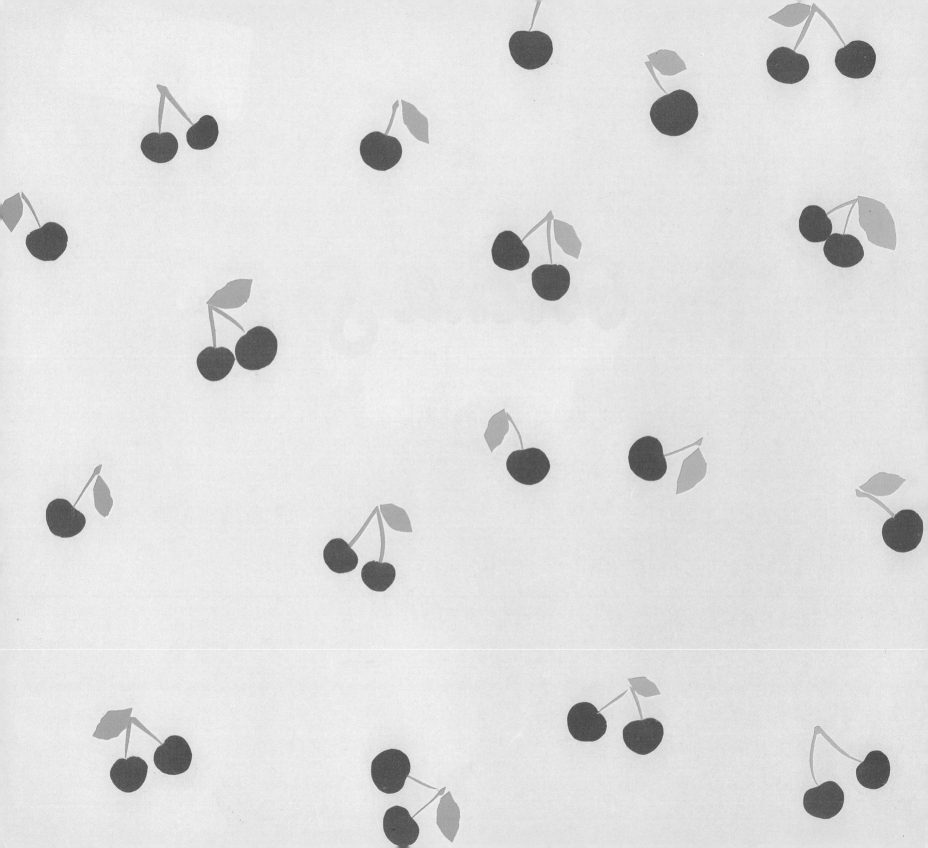

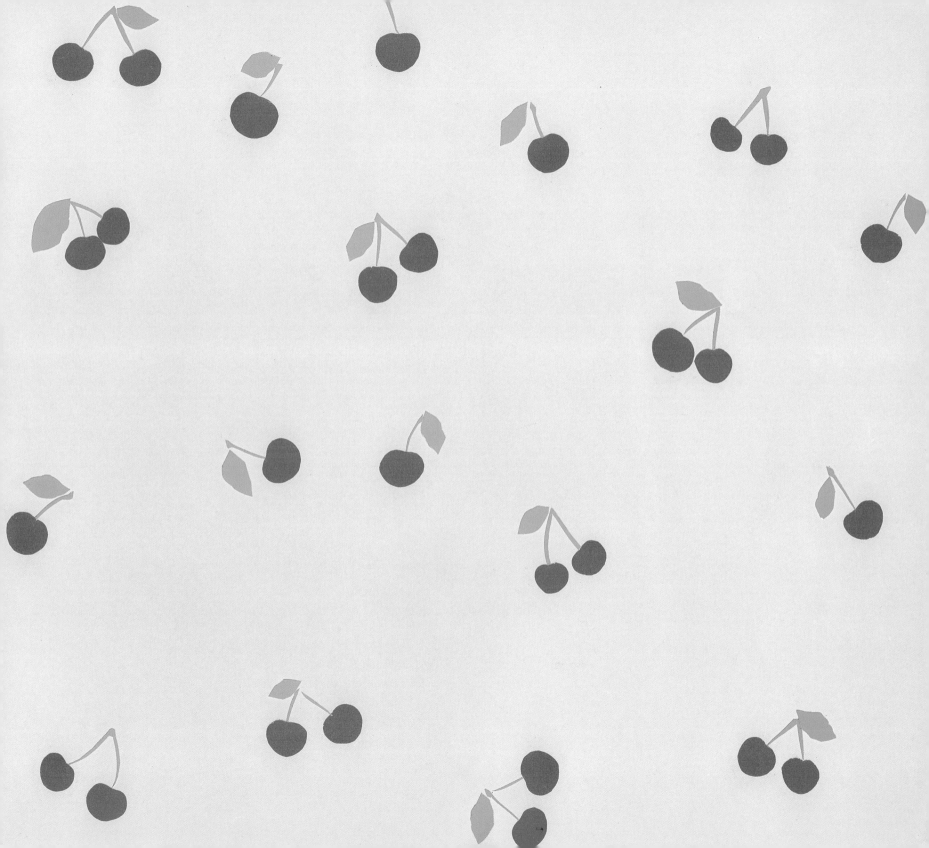

To Amelia and Harriet
A.A.

To Luke and Jason
R.P.M

ORCHARD BOOKS
96 Leonard Street, London EC2A 4XD
Orchard Books Australia
14 Mars Road, Lane Cove, NSW 2066
1 86039 064 1 (hardback)
1 86039 951 7 (paperback)
First published in Great Britain in 1998
This edition published in 1999
A CIP catalogue record for this book is available from the British Library.
1 3 5 7 9 10 8 6 4 2 (hardback)
3 5 7 9 10 8 6 4 2 (paperback)
Printed in Belgium.

The Gotcha Smile

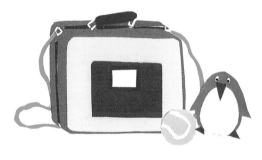

* Rita Phillips Mitchell *

* Alex Ayliffe *

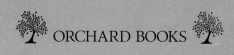

ORCHARD BOOKS

Today was a special day for Clarine. It was her first day at her new school.

Clarine wanted to make lots of friends.

"Children, this is Clarine, our new pupil," said Miss Green.

The morning started with painting.

"I like to draw people best," said Clarine. "This is my Mum."

"Hey!" said Lisa. "You jogged my arm and made me mess up my picture."

"I didn't mean to," cried Clarine.

At playtime Miss Green took Clarine outside.
"Lisa, look after Clarine, please. She doesn't
know anyone yet, so let her join in with you."
But Lisa ran off to play with her friends.

"I don't like school," said Clarine on her way home.

"Why, what happened today?" asked her Mum.

"I didn't make any friends," said Clarine.

"Oh, that'll come soon enough," said Mum.
"And remember, I'll always be your friend."

"You're different. I mean friends
who are little like me."

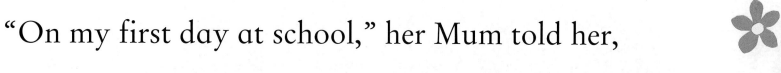

"On my first day at school," her Mum told her,

"I shared my apples with another little girl.
Her name was Pam."

The next day at playtime, Clarine got out a bag
of shiny red cherries her Mum had given her.
"Do you want some of my cherries?"
she called to Lisa and her friends.
Quick as a flash a little crowd gathered round her,
pushing and calling out for the cherries.
"Now I've lots of friends," she said to herself.

But soon the cherries were all gone
and so were the new friends.

"How was school today?" asked her Dad that evening. And Clarine told him all about the cherries.

"A little chatterbox like you will make friends in no time, just wait and see," said her father.

"How did you make friends when you were little, Dad?" she asked.

Her father smiled. "Well, I had this special ball.

I took it everywhere. So when I started school, it came too and all the boys wanted to play with me."

The next day Clarine took a ball
to school with her. At playtime,
she bounced the ball around. She
bounced it so high it went on the roof.
"I've lost my ball," said Clarine
to some boys. "Can I play with you?"

"Later," said Stuart.
"We're in the middle
of a game now."

But Clarine caught
their ball and ran off.
They chased her round
and round until Clarine
gave it back.

"What's the matter with my little schoolgirl?" asked Clarine's
Grandpa that afternoon.

"I'm not a schoolgirl any more, Grandpa," said Clarine,
"'cos I'm never going back!"

And Clarine told him about the boys.

"Running off with their
ball isn't going to make friends,"
said Grandpa.

"I won't go back,"
said Clarine. "No one
wants to play with me!"

"Well now, let me see," said Clarine's Grandpa.
"When I was little I had the brightest smile
you ever did see.

And when I shot that smile at anyone they just
had to shoot one right back. I used to call it
my Gotcha Smile. Why don't you give it a try?"

"I could *try* smiling," said Clarine.

"Sure," said her Grandpa. "And you know what, you have a Gotcha Smile too. When you smile at me, I can't do anything else but smile right back."

Both Clarine and Grandpa started to chuckle and chuckle.

Then Clarine's Grandpa said, "Look, Clarine, why don't you go back to school and finish off the week, eh? Just for me."

"All right then. I'll go back…just for you," said Clarine.

"That's my girl," said Grandpa.

The next day at playtime Clarine watched some children playing basketball. Suddenly the ball came flying towards her, and she caught it up in her arms as Glen came chasing after it. Without thinking, Clarine shot Glen her Gotcha Smile.

"Can I have a go?" she asked.

"OK, go on then," said Glen.
Clarine bounced the ball...

...one
...two...three.
Then she threw it
as high as she could.
Wham! The ball went right through the net.

"Great!" shouted everybody.

"Come and play on our side," shouted Lisa. Then Clarine remembered what her Grandpa had told her and she shot her Gotcha Smile at Lisa. Would you believe it, Lisa fired one right back.

"I'm sorry I spoilt your picture the other day.
I just wanted to be your friend," said Clarine.

"I'd like to be your friend, too," said Lisa.

That afternoon Grandpa was waiting for Clarine at
the school gates. "I like school Grandpa, and even when
I'm as old as you I'll still keep right on going," said Clarine.

"The Gotcha Smile worked, then, did it?" he said.

"And guess what, Grandpa, I've found a friend who
has a Gotcha Smile, too! Her name is Lisa."

And Grandpa and Clarine smiled their very biggest

Gotcha Smiles.

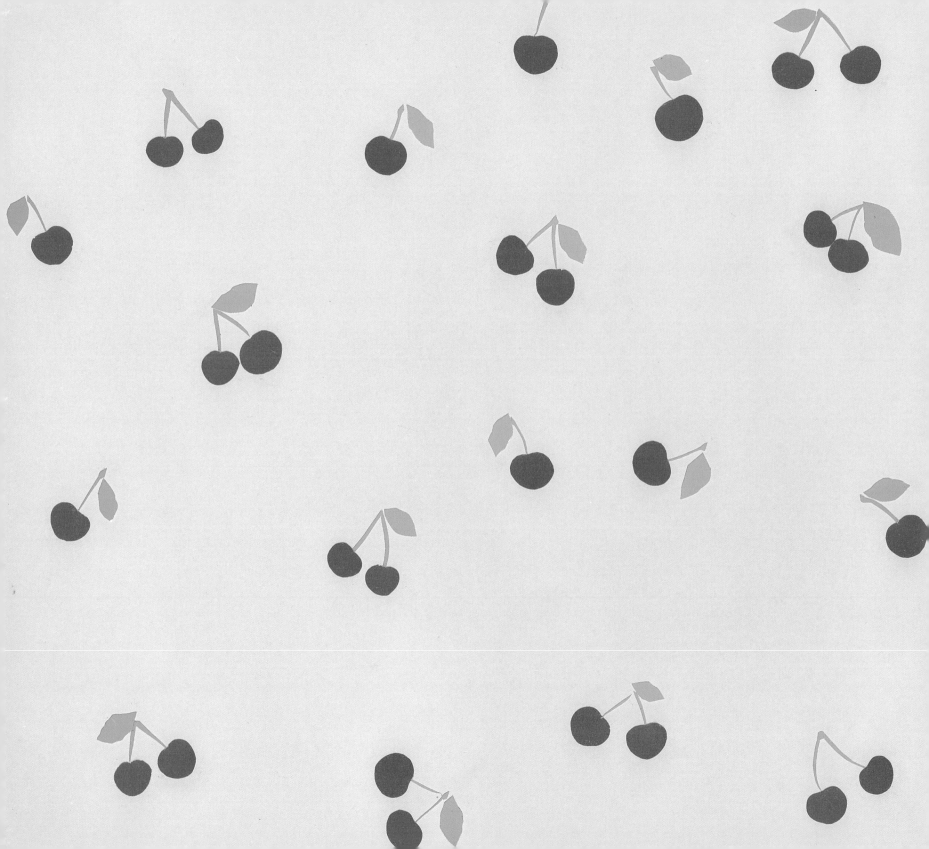

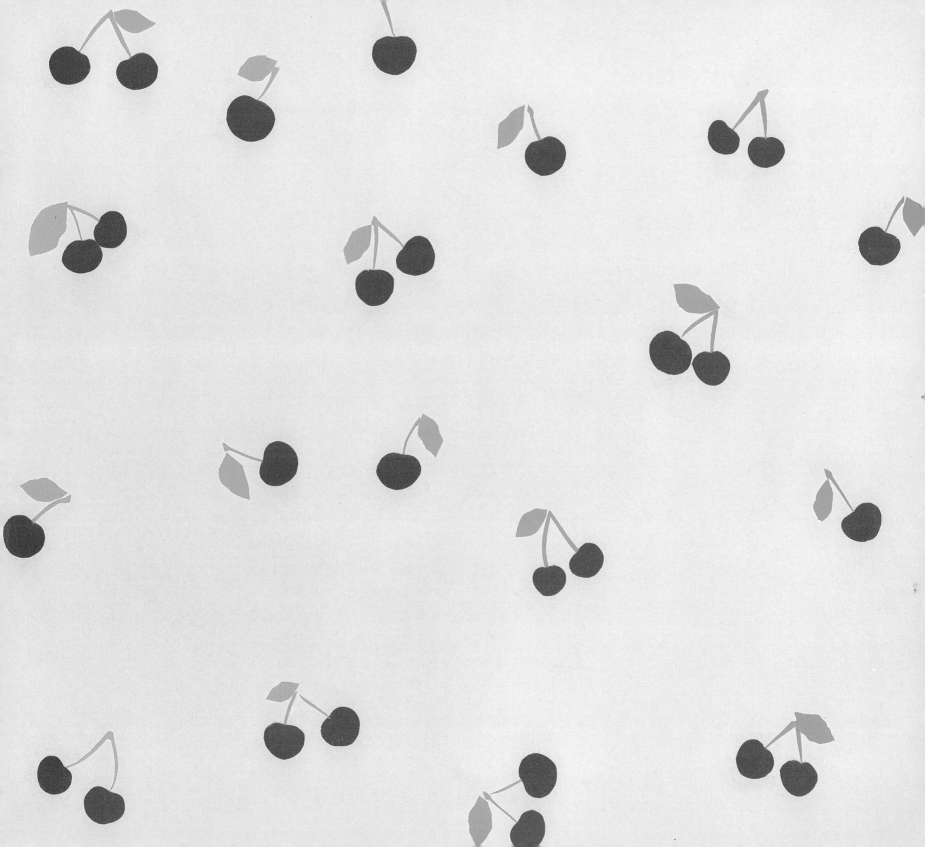